To Diane

What great fun to meet you in Hays. I'll look forward to our next visit. Until then,

Best Wishes,

David Hanson

October 12, 1996

For Jule and Jon, two great reasons
why families are so wonderful.

Love, D. H.

To my kissing cousin, Harry Fred Bigler,
and the Shawville power plant.

—B.L.

Text copyright © 1996 by David L. Harrison
Illustrations copyright © 1996 by Betsy Lewin

Published by Wordsong
Boyds Mills Press, Inc.
A Highlights Company
815 Church Street
Honesdale, Pennsylvania 18431
Printed in Mexico

Publisher Cataloging-in-Publication Data
Harrison, David L.
    A thousand cousins / poems of family life by David L. Harrison ;
illustrated by Betsy Lewin.—1st ed.
[32]p. : col. ill. ; cm.
Summary : A collection of humorous poems about family life and
relationships accompanied by colorful cartoon-like illustrations.
ISBN 1-56397-131-3
1. Family life—Children's poetry. 2. Children's poetry, American.
[1. Family life—Poetry. 2. Poetry, American.] I. Lewin, Betsy, ill.
II. Title.
811.54—dc20   1996   AC
Library of Congress Catalog Card Number 94-79158

First edition, 1996
Book designed by Charlotte Staub
The text of this book is set in 14-point Clarendon Light.
The illustrations are done in pen and ink and watercolors.
Distributed by St. Martin's Press

10 9 8 7 6 5 4 3 2 1

A THOUSAND COUSINS

Poems of Family Life

by David L. Harrison

Illustrated by Betsy Lewin

WORDSONG

Boyds Mills Press

CONTENTS

A THOUSAND COUSINS

Where did I get these cousins?
I never ordered any.
What earthly good are cousins?
And why are there so many?
I bet I've got a thousand
I'd sell you for a penny.

WHO ATE THE LAST FIVE COOKIES?

My sister said, "I couldn't!"
So I said, "I'm sure you could."

She said, "I really shouldn't!"
And I said, "I think you should."

She said, "You know I wouldn't!"
But I said, "I bet you would."

So when she said, "I didn't!"
I said, "Mama, yes she did!"

I was bad and I admit it.
(Just don't tell her where I've hid.)

THE DIFFERENCE

My father'd never bother
To make me scrub
In the tub.
He wouldn't care
If I didn't comb my hair
Or put on clean underwear.
He'd never choose my shoes
To match my shirt,
And he sure wouldn't
Check my neck
For dirt
Or make a guy
Put on a tie.
So why do you suppose
I smell like a rose,
And I'm gussied up
Like the sissiest buttercup
You ever saw?

'Cause of Ma.

MAMAS

✖

Who says mamas make the rules?
Who put them in charge?
How come mamas act like they just know?
I don't have to mind my mama,
I'm not afraid of her!
"Comin' Mama!"
Sorry, I gotta go.

NOT TONIGHT!

Do the dishes?
Me?
Tonight?
I've got three whole books to read!
Yeah, right!
Plus two reports
That are twelve miles long,
And if you think that's all,
You're wrong!
There's my dumb piano,
My hair's a mess,
So see!
Somebody answer that phone!
For me?
Hi, Tim!
A movie?
Great!
In twenty minutes?
Sure!
Don't be late!

PRACTICE

Since Mama bought this stupid horn
I hate the day that I was born
'Cause nothing makes me more forlorn
Than practice practice practice.
Other guys are playing ball
But Mama doesn't care at all,
She's going to drive me up the wall
With practice practice practice.
I deserve to go to jail
For murdering this B flat scale
And sounding like a dying whale
From practice practice practice.
I tried to tell her I'm not bright
So I could practice half the night
Forever and not get it right,
Why practice practice practice?
But nothing helps, not even tears,
I'm doomed to play this horn for years
With Mama yelling in my ears,
PRACTICE PRACTICE PRACTICE!

DADDY'S SNORE

I try to fall asleep before
My daddy starts his nightly snore,
For once he does you can't ignore
The chain saw sound of Daddy's snore.
The ocean pounding on the shore
Has nothing on my daddy's snore.
The lion with his mighty roar
Is a pussycat to Daddy's snore.
Daddy's mother always swore
She tried to teach him not to snore.
Mama says, "It's quite a chore
To be so close to Daddy's snore."
My sister says, "I just abhore
The way our father loves to snore."
My brother slams his bedroom door
And yells, "I hate that awful snore!"
Our neighbors say, "It's such a bore
Listening to your father snore."
I've counted sheep and walked the floor
And stuffed my ears with cotton galore.
It's fifteen minutes after four,
I cannot stand this anymore.
I love my daddy to the core,
But I've got to have some silence or
I'm never going to learn to snore.

A LONG NIGHT

Something's in my closet!
It's growly!
  Snarly!
  Creepy!
"Daddy! Daddy!"
  "Turn off your light."
"Mama!"
  "Everything's all right."
Boy, is this going to be a long night.
I'm DEFINITELY
 not
  sleepy.

HE'LL PAY FOR THIS!

✂

Here I stand, forlorn and bare,
My brother hid my underwear,
I cannot find them anywhere,
So close the door!
It's rude to stare!

I JUST CAN'T TELL

Daddy says I have pitcher ears
And a cowlick in my hair,
Brother calls me a monkey
With a skunk in my underwear,
Mama says I'm a silly goose
And as stubborn as a goat,
And Sister says I grow like a weed
And talk like a motorboat,
Grandma says I eat like a horse
But I'm her little lamb,
So I don't know if I'm fish or fowl
Or exactly what I am.

WE DON'T LIKE TO TALK ABOUT IT

"My sister wanted a prince so bad
She actually kissed a frog!"
  "Did the frog turn into a prince?"
"No, my sister turned into a frog.

Turned out the frog was not a prince
But an evil witch in disguise."
  "Did she make your sister a girl again?"
"Yes, but she's fond of flies."

THE SAD TALE OF JONATHAN WHO
WOULDN'T EAT HIS VEGETABLES

Jonathan hated vegetables,
I mean he HATED vegetables!
"I'll NEVER eat a vegetable,"
He said, "of any kind!"
"You won't grow up," our mother sighed.
She served them boiled and stewed and fried,
But Jonathan said, "I won't! I won't!
And you can't make me mind!"

Every day our sister, Sue,
Said, "Vegetables are good for you!
You won't grow up without them."
But he said, "I'd rather die!"
"Try some, Jonathan," begged our dad,
"These vegetables are not so bad."
But Jonathan cried, "I hate them!
You'll never make me try!"

"You won't grow up," our brother said,
But nothing got through Jonathan's head.
He kicked and screamed and pitched a fit
And drove the family wild.
And so it grieves me to report
That Jonathan met the saddest sort
Of fate because he wouldn't eat
His veggies as a child.

Our friends all gobbled vegetables,
They slurped and swallowed vegetables,
And that's the reason, I suppose,
They grew up one and all.
While Jonathan, as I'm sure you know,
Never did begin to grow,
And now he's ninety-seven,
But he's only two feet tall.

WHAT MAKES IT ALL WORTHWHILE

I do my homework every night,
I climb in bed by nine,
I say "Yes, ma'am" and "No, sir,"
And I never beg or whine.
I make my bed
And clean my room
And hang my clothes away.
I shine my shoes
And wash my hair
And shower every day.
Mama says that I'm as good
As any son could be,
And Daddy tells my brother
To try to be more like me,
Which makes my brother crazy,
Which makes me sweetly smile,
Which makes him scream,
"I'll get you for this!"
Which makes being good worthwhile.

SNUG

Mama and Papa
And we fourteen kids
Moved into this sparrow nest,
But Mama's expecting
Twins again,
So none of us gets much rest.

BUDDIES

When Grandpa winks,
I wink.
When he giggles,
I giggle.
When his tummy
Feels rumbly,
My tummy
Feels rumbly.
I don't know how Grandpa
Got to be
So much like me,
But he is.
Maybe he's old enough
To act my age,
Maybe I'm young enough
To act his.

SHE WAS RIGHT!

Sister said, "I'm sugar-sweet,
If I got wet, I'd melt."
I knew I shouldn't oughta,
But I hosed her down with water.
Now all that's left of Sister
Are her tennies and her belt.

OUR LITTLE BROTHER

Our little brother's name is Paul
Bartholomew Frockmorton
William Jennings Lincoln
Alexander Jackson Horton
Richard Lyndon Timothy
Leonardo Jeffrey Sid
Edward Perry Johnson,
But we just call him kid,
'Cause by the time you holler, "Paul
Bartholomew Frockmorton
William Jennings Lincoln
Alexander Jackson Horton
Richard Lyndon Timothy
Leonardo Jeffrey Sid
Edward Perry, OPEN THE DOOR!"
You're sorry that you did.

SECONDHAND

My shirt?
Belonged to my brother.
My pants?
My brother's, too.
My shoes? Socks? Underwear?
What do you think, they're new?
My hair?
Same as my sister's.
My eyes?
Mama's blue.
My name?
They call me Junior, of course,
But I expect you already knew.

FAMILY SECRETS

✄

My aunt thinks she's a mallard duck,
It's sort of hard to explain,
But don't go eat at her house
'Cause all she serves is grain.

FIRST THINGS FIRST

Grandma hates my loud music,
Drive-in restaurants,
And not getting to bed before
The late news has begun.
She likes yucky green salads,
Pulling weeds,
Putting things away,
And getting up before the sun.
Mama says when I grow up
I may be more like Grandma,
But first things first,
I just dug a worm,
And I'm going fishing with Grandpa.

MY BABY UNCLE

I have a baby uncle
Who was just born last night,
I know he's really my uncle,
But it doesn't feel quite right.
An uncle should be older
And be married to an aunt.
You want my baby uncle?
Fine!
You'll have to change his pants.

HA-HA-HA, HE HAD TO

Brother hated raking leaves,
But Mama said he had to,
"It's your responsibility," she said,
"You should be glad to."
Brother shook his head and said,
"I really think it's bad to
Waste my time on dumb old leaves,
I'd much prefer for Dad to."
But Dad said, "Son, raking leaves
Is a good way for a lad to
Learn to help around the house.
It shouldn't make you sad to
Work a little now and then."

It sure made Brother mad to
Rake and pick up all those leaves,
But ha-ha-ha, he had to!

YOU CAN'T HAVE TOO MANY

My daddy works in an office,
And Daddy's daddy grew up on a farm,
And Daddy's daddy's daddy shot a buffalo,
And Daddy's daddy's daddy's daddy skinned a beaver
To make Daddy's daddy's daddy's mother a hat.
And Daddy's daddy's daddy's daddy's daddy
Married an Indian girl named Jenny,
And Daddy's daddy's daddy's daddy's daddy's daddy...
What?
That's a lot of Daddy's daddies?
Well, you just can't have too many.